Wee Witch

POLISHES THE
STARS

ANNE OGILVIE DUFF

PAGE PUBLISHING, INC.
Conneaut Lake, PA

First originally published by Page Publishing 2020

ISBN 978-1-64628-487-0 (pbk)
ISBN 978-1-64628-488-7 (digital)

Printed in the United States of America

For Erica, who asked, "Tell me a story."

Once upon a time, by a twisty-turny stream at the edge of the Magic Forest, a Wee Witch lived in a willow tree with branches, which went this way and that.

The willow leaves whished in the whispery wind.

The twisty-turny stream trickled and sang.

Hidden in the lumpy, bumpy roots of the willow tree was her little arched door with a window of glinting green glass. On a hook behind the door hung a cloak, a pointy hat, and a do-good bag.

3

Every night, when the sun had set and the clouds had lost their pink, the Wee Witch picked up her do-good bag with soft, silky polishing cloths and a bottle of iridescent star shine. She put on her cloak and her pointy hat, opened her little arched door, and jumped on her wee broomstick.

The Wee Witch shot up, up, far into the sky, across the big round moon, until she reached the farthest star. Her do-good bag hung nicely over a tippy point. She got to work with her wee broom, sweeping soft cobwebs caught in the sparkles and polishing the star until it twinkled. Off she flew to the next star, brushing and polishing until it sparkled and shone. All night long, she flitted from star to star, cleaning and shining with her soft cloths.

Far, far below,
the twisty-turny
stream
trickled
and sang,

the willow leaves whispered, and the Magic Forest stretched
for ever and ever…but not quite.

6

On the other side of the Magic Forest, there was a city, all hustle and bustle. People rushed, ran, pushed, shoved, and hurried from place to place. Cars whizzed down streets, making an awful noise. Truck engines roared, cars honked their horns. Clouds of smoke

and dust rose up to the sky, covering the moon in a curtain of gray; covering the stars so they ceased to sparkle at all. People had forgotten to look up; they had forgotten there were stars.

A child noticed first. She looked out of her window at the big yellow moon.

She saw the sky.

"LOOK! LOOK UP!" she said.

One by one, the busy people in the city looked up. They laughed and smiled. They could see a whole sky of twinkling stars.

Look! Look up!

Hurray!

Only the child noticed the Wee Witch with her do-good bag
of soft polishing cloths and star shine, gliding across the moon.

12

Just as the first rays of morning sunshine broke through the brightening horizon, the Wee Witch polished the last star, the littlest and brightest of all, and gathered up her do-good bag.

Exhausted, the Wee Witch returned to her home under the willow tree with branches, which went this way and that, by the twisty-turny stream at the edge of the Magic Forest. She propped her wee broom by her little arched door with the glinting green glass window, went inside, and jumped into bed.

Sleep well, Wee Witch. Good night.

The End

ABOUT THE AUTHOR

Anne Ogilvie Duff is an artist and a storyteller. She grew up in Scotland and graduated from Edinburgh College of Art before coming to the United States. She taught in the Fine Arts department at Culver Academies in Indiana for twenty-two years. She has illustrated poetry and prose, including *JT Owl Learns to Share* by Dana S. Neer.

Anne loves nature and spends much of her time on long walks by Lake Maxinkuckee, especially with her six grandchildren. She lives in Culver, Indiana.